Fausterella and other stories

By Kate Harrad

Copyright 2011 Kate Harrad

ISBN: 978-1-4477-5968-3

A Lulu publication

www.lulu.com

The Winter Tree was previously published by Shimmer magazine. *Stepmother* was previously published by ken*again. *They're Not Dead Until They Stop Talking* was previously published by Lenox Avenue. *The Soho Puppeteer* was previously published by Dark Tales. Thanks to all of them for permission to republish.

The cover photo was taken by Simon MacMullen. Thanks to him and to the model, our friend Jessamy, for permission to use it; and thanks to Trish for proofreading the stories.

Kate's website is at loveandzombies.co.uk.

Contents

~~~~~~~~

They're Not Dead Until They Stop Talking

There was a ghost in the machine.

But the machine was only an electric toothbrush. And the ghost was too recently dead to be a threat to anyone. She had passed away the day before, and what she was doing in the toothbrush was anyone's guess.

Certainly I didn't know. My grandmother had been normal all her life and we had every reason to expect that she would be as conventional a ghost as the rest of the family. I know for a fact that my grandfather was decidedly disappointed in her.

"What the bloody hell is she doing in there?" I could hear him muttering to himself as he wandered up and down in the kitchen cupboard. "Didn't she want to see me any more? God knows there's enough space in the oven. We could have been in the same room for eternity. I would have had time to tell her all about my war experiences again." Grandpa had been too young for World War 2, but he had lived through Vietnam, albeit 6,000 miles away in a neutral country. He had always enjoyed relating his memories of watching the news throughout the '60s.

Personally I was pleased with Grandmother's choice of home. I had never used the toothbrush much, whereas Grandpa's kitchen cupboard was needed for plates and saucers, which I was currently having to keep in the fridge. (It wasn't that they inconvenienced him, but after a few days in there they had traces of ectoplasm, and a ghoulish film settled on all the food.) Of course Great-Aunt Hilda was in the fridge, but she didn't seem to leak quite so much. And she had far better manners.

I did have a couple of rooms to myself. Nobody was allowed to live in my bedroom except me, and my bathroom was also out of bounds. The ghosts had the main bathroom, a couple of bedrooms and the living-room - and the kitchen because I couldn't stop them. They seemed to feel better in there, it being warmer and cosier than the rest of the house: occasionally they'd cook for me but it was always burnt. Only someone with a ghost's skewed sense of cuisine could burn lettuce.

No, they didn't scare me. Ghosts are ghosts, and they're just like humans only more transparent. Ghosts have intelligence, and they don't move much... and they have just the two legs, and they don't scuttle at you... well, it should be obvious that what scared me - the only thing that scared me in the house - were spiders. We had lots of them because they liked the ectoplasm: it made them bigger, blacker and, strangely, better at scuttling. Great-uncle Henry encouraged them, I know.

"They're just insects with spare legs, Jamie," he said in what he thought were reassuring tones. "Why should you be frightened of eight legs but not of six?"

"I'm frightened of six legs as well, Uncle Henry. I'm just thirty-three per cent more scared of eight."

"They're more scared of you than you are of them."

"That's not possible."

And as the only live person in the house, I was assigned the task of cleaning it, thereby dislodging anything that happened to be, for example, weaving a web in the corner of the ceiling. Actually, that indirectly solved the problem; at least for a while. When a spider fell on my head once, I shut myself in my room and refused to come out until somebody had done something about either a) the spiders or b) my fear of them. Two days later I emerged to find that, by some ghostly magic, the house was completely free of anything with more than two legs. It was much later when Henry finally confessed to me that he had just sprayed the whole house with insect killer, and kept doing it every night for the next two years. Which explained the symptoms of poisoning that I had assumed were due to the cooking.

My great-aunt Hilda was a problem too. It was widely maintained in the family (particularly by Henry, who had been married to her) that her preference for living in the refrigerator was related to her notorious chilliness in life. I didn't remember her alive, except for a faint memory from when I was three, of someone trying to pat me on the head and failing to make contact. Hilda liked, on the whole, to be left alone. We liked, on the whole, to leave her alone. But I did pat her head every time I took the margarine out. A wincing ghost makes a good fridge magnet, that's my motto - though I can see it wouldn't work for everyone.

Grandmother seemed happy in the toothbrush, but we worried about her. Well, I worried about her: my dead relatives were more inclined to think about the quality of live people these days and how much more fun haunting used to be. When you die you just get older.

I worried about all of them. Whether Grandpa was happy in the cupboard, and whether he needed more people to talk to - he'd started lecturing the salt shaker about the dangers of Communism and his belief that not enough people wore slippers. Whether Henry really enjoyed haunting or just went through the motions: he'd actually begun to wear a white sheet with a hole in it, which looks especially odd on a headless see-through ghost. Perhaps all of them needed more people to haunt, not just me. I tried to look scared when they leapt out on me, but it had stopped being convincing twenty years ago. Four apparitions to one person isn't good for anyone: I was starting to feel a bit transparent myself. Since the spiders had gone I didn't have much to remind me of reality. Not that I wanted them back, with their spiky blackness and their malicious scuttling - better a boring life than one filled with terror. Still, living with four dead relatives wasn't my idea of a good time. It had probably never been anyone's.

It all happened thirty years ago, when I was fifteen. I was, if I say so myself, a moderately attractive teenager, or would have been if we'd invented the word. A wizard wanted to marry me. Well, that was how we described it, I don't think any wedding ceremonies would have actually ensued. "Be mine," was the way he put it, being a bit poetic. No indication of my future prospects after I'd been his, which I frankly regarded as a bad sign.

Let's be honest, he tried to get me into bed. But I was a strong and very determined girl with a sharp set of knuckles: he was never quite the same again, and definitely spoke in more of a falsetto.

I was feisty, you see.

High-spirited.

Stupid.

He cursed me to be haunted by all the blood relatives of mine who died during my life. No, not very relevant to the offence I agree, some would have just hypnotised me into bed and kept me there till I died of pleasure. Now I come to think about it, it might not have been such a bad life. But no, he chose the bizarre option. Apparently it was the only curse he knew how to do properly.

With four ghosts living in the house, my marriage prospects became so tiny you could have accidentally trodden on them without even noticing. My parents died when I was twenty-five, of frustration. With a touch of ectoplasm poisoning. A very intelligent revenge, now I come to think of it, on the part of the Great Magnifico. (Yes, I know, but he did children's parties and old people's homes as well as lifelong evil curses and non-consensual seduction.)

I had a talk to my grandmother, about whether she was really happy in the toothbrush: wasn't it a bit small for her, anyway? She claimed to be fine, mentioning something about the nice vibrations when she turned the electricity on. It was clear that she didn't need Grandpa any more, though she seemed to have a yearning to see Henry. I sent him along, with the small occasional table under which he lived, and tried to ignore the sound of the toothbrush banging up and down on the pine table top. Neither of them would ever talk about it.

I wasn't sure I could stand it any more.

In the end it was the spiders that solved everything. I would have got the ghosts exorcised years ago, you see, if it hadn't been for two things: my concern for their feelings, and my disinclination to live in the house on my own, with the spiders. Then Henry ran out of insect killer, two years after promising he'd get rid of them. So he confessed his method to me. I'd thought he used some ghoulish thing only ghosts knew how to do, and all the time he'd been doing something I could have done myself - if I hadn't been so dependant on him. It was my epiphany - you know when someone's been looking after their elderly mother or whatever all their life, and then they die and the person finds out they could get along perfectly well without them? Or they just pine away and die, but that's not the point. The point is, I realised I didn't need my relatives. And I didn't feel responsible for them any more. Hilda with her fridge and her terror of physical contact even now that she couldn't feel any. Grandpa with his insane war stories ("War is hell. I should know, I've listened to enough radio broadcasts."). Henry and Grandmother with their strange secret goings-on; I had been forced to move the occasional table into the bathroom, and lay awake at night trying not to hear the clattering. Even dead people had a better sex life than me. What on earth could I owe them? I had been cursed enough. I ordered a priest.

The priest, it turned out, was none other than the Great Magnifico. I'd forgotten wizards don't die - not until they want to - and he'd obviously forgotten all about me. He'd been to America at some point, too.

"Gee Jamie, I'm sorry. You should have got in touch. You know how it is, these things happen, you get angry, you do things you regret later - "

"And then you remember to take the curse away and let the person lead a normal life. Unless, that is , you move to the other side of the world and forget about it." I was not happy.

"I'll make it up to you."

"I'm forty-five. I can't think of anything you could possibly do to make it up to me."

"I guess you're right. How about free tickets to The Great Magnifico's Reincarnation and Therapy Session, once a month at the Pagan Holistic New Age Healing and Hypnotism Centre, guaranteed success or your past life back?"

"Thanks, but I just want some peace and quiet. And preferably never to hear another ghost having sex."

"Can do." He smiled widely; he'd clearly had his teeth widened and whitened somewhere along the line. "Anything for you, Jamie darlin'. You know I always had a bit of a thing for you."

"No, really?"

"Oh yes," he leered. Even the ghosts understood irony better than this man.

But he gave me a new wonder product for the spiders, and my relatives have gone for good. The traces of ectoplasm never washed out though, and I can never use the toothbrush or the table again. I can't help wondering if I'll meet them all again when I die.

Some people dread that there won't be an afterlife.

I'm just afraid that I know exactly what it's going to be like.

~~~~~

The Soho Puppeteer

"I want a puppet," said my boyfriend Phil.

"Sorry?" The remark was out of context: we'd been lying in bed silently reading the papers for half an hour, and he'd never mentioned any puppet-related cravings before.

He pointed to a small advert in the back of *Private Eye*, which we'd bought because the election was coming up and we wanted to know what was really going on behind the scenes (but I'd ended up reading *Cosmo* instead because it had an interview with Christian Bale). There was a black-and-white picture of a cheerful clown on strings above an address: *The Soho Puppeteer, Wardour Street*. Nothing else, but I suppose nothing else was really needed. I was mildly impressed with the economy of information.

"It's just reminded me," said Phil in an explanatory fashion, "my drama class wants one. It's a useful exercise apparently. You have to make something else act, you see, displace all the physical energy onto the puppet. Teaches you a lot about precision and control."

I had been paying for Phil's drama class for two years now. I still believed him when he said he was certain it was paying off and a thriving career in the soaps - or possibly in the serious theatre - was imminent. Now and then I thought about asking him to get a proper job, even a part-time one, just to help with the bills, but I knew he'd talk me out of the idea after five minutes; he was good at that, very persuasive. The easiest route was just to go along with what he wanted. It wasn't that hard: he was sweet, fun and intelligent, even if he did get a bit actor-y at times.

"Sounds interesting," I said. "Why don't you go along this afternoon and get one?"

"Can't afford it."

"I meant I'd buy it, obviously. I've got to pick up some food first, but I'll meet you in the shop around three."

"Thank you, sweetie." Phil leaned over to kiss my hand. "I think it'll really help. I'm having trouble getting my body to be properly responsive. It's all there in my head, I just need to get it out, you know?"

"I know."

Soho on a Saturday afternoon wasn't as busy as Oxford Street, which was just north of it, but it was a lot more interesting. When I'd first moved to London three years earlier I'd kept fascinated track of how many piercings, outrageous tattoos and bizarre hairstyles I could count just walking from Tottenham Court Road to Charing Cross. Of course, at that point I was also noticing every black person, every obvious gay man, and anybody who was wearing fishnets; I'd grown up in Devon and the multicoloured variety of the city was endlessly absorbing to me. Now I'd sort of got over it, but I still got a tiny thrill whenever I saw two men holding hands or a butch woman with a metal ball through her lip. The shops in Soho gave me a similar feeling of sophistication, especially the ones in Old Compton Street with the flyers for the fetish clubs and the purple leather harnesses with the interesting straps.

Wardour Street, at the end of Old Compton Street, went down to Shaftsbury Avenue and up to Oxford Street. I wondered which way to go and opted for walking north. In midafternoon the sex show signs looked dim and embarrassed, though I noticed they were still attracting customers. The women sitting on the stools by the signs didn't try to entice me in; wrong gender. I felt vaguely affronted.

Sex shop, strip club, newsagent, trendy sushi restaurant, strip club, sex shop, enormous crowded pub. I'd walked up here before and didn't remember seeing a puppet shop, but there it was, a tiny concrete storefront trapped between the enormous pub and a particularly dingy sex shop. The Soho Puppeteer. There was barely room for the name above the door. I checked my watch: just after three. Good. I liked being on time.

The shop was narrow but surprisingly long, though I realised it wasn't surprising at all given how large its neighbours were; of course there would be more space than there appeared from the outside. It wasn't very well lit, but well enough to allow me to see the profusion of puppets lining every shelf and hanging from every scrap of ceiling. Wooden, fabric and plastic faces peered down at me in shades of happiness, misery, cruelty, greed, yearning and a hundred other variations of emotion. Impressive. Their costumes were good too, some in military uniforms, some in ball gowns, some dressed as policemen or cooks or cardinals, some just in colourful clothes or plain black. Looking around and up I felt dizzy, and closed my eyes for a moment.

When I opened them I realised what was missing from the shop: Phil. I didn't bother to be surprised, since he was always exactly fifteen minutes late for everything all the time. In fact, there was nobody else in the shop except for the man behind the counter, who was watching me impassively. He was black and also dressed in black, which made him almost invisible in the dim light. I wondered why they didn't make it brighter. Maybe the puppets weren't as well-made as they looked and they were hoping customers wouldn't noticed until they'd

12

bought one and left the shop with it. If so, they'd probably underestimated the canniness of central London shoppers, I thought.

"Can I help you?" The shopkeeper's voice was very low, with no accent I could place. I gave my standard answer - "Just browsing, thanks," - and picked up a puppet at random from the shelf beside me, to confirm that I was a legitimate customer. It was the clown from the Private Eye advert. I don't like clowns, but I didn't want to look unappreciative, so I held it for a minute before putting it down and picking up another one, a judge. Its grey wig felt rough against my hand.

Maybe I should choose a puppet for Phil. After all, I was paying for it. What would be a good choice for his drama class? Nothing too specific, or it would limit him. One of the non-uniformed ones. I spotted a wooden figure on one of the top shelves wearing jeans and a white T-shirt: how cute! I knew I couldn't reach it, though.

"Excuse me." I approached the back of the shop where the shop assistant (owner? manager?) sat. "Could I look at that one?" I pointed vaguely, to indicate that it was too high for my reach.

"Certainly." I expected him to get up, but he didn't. He pressed something on the desk in front of him, and the dark wooden door behind him opened to reveal a tall pale black-clad man, well over six feet, who glided noiselessly past me and plucked down the jeans-and-teeshirt puppet, handed it to me, and disappeared back through the door. I was a little spooked, but the puppet was delightful: cheeky grin, hair that felt real, little black leather shoes, and the jeans were very thin denim, so that they felt the right texture for his size.

"How much is it?"

"Fifty pounds."

I gulped, but I'd been expecting about that much. I handed over my debit card. The shopkeeper held it for a moment, then gave it back to me. "We don't take cards." He was wearing black gloves and his hands looked enormous, or at least the fingers did. Did he have some kind of deformity? I wasn't about to ask.

"Do you take cheques?"

"Just cash."

"Right. I'll be back in a few minutes, then."

"OK." He put my puppet on the counter, where it sat impishly swinging its legs. They really were well-made, I thought. Well worth the money.

The cash point wasn't where I'd thought it was. In fact, all the cash points seemed to have been removed from Soho. Maybe it was an anti-crime measure, or maybe nobody got cash out any more because everywhere took cards. Everywhere except puppet shops. I went round a corner and another corner and realised I'd got myself turned around. I was close to Wardour Street, I thought, but I couldn't find it. I turned down a narrow alley more or less at random, and recognised the big chain pub next to the Soho Puppeteer. Right, so I was behind the shop; that yard must belong to it. Maybe there was a back way in. I pushed open the door to the yard, which was full of rubble and wires, and peered in at a window. The curtains were drawn but there was a couple of inches' gap I could see through. At this point I was just curious, really, because clearly this wasn't a customer entrance. I peered in.

The back room of the shop was much brighter than the shop itself, and decorated in pale rather than dark colours, with no decoration. There were benches around the edge of the room like a school gym, and four shop assistants were sitting on them, one on each side. They were wearing black like the man who'd reached down my puppet - in fact, I thought he was one of the men in the room, but it was hard to be sure because they all looked similar. All tall, all pale and all blank-looking. Their black suits were stark against the light brown of the benches. None of them were moving, not even shifting position.

I saw all of this, but I didn't remember any of it till afterwards, because the most immediately noticeable feature of the room and of the men was this: they all had dark wires attached to their shoulders. And the wires went up to the ceiling, which had wires running along it in several directions. I made a small high-pitched sound in the back of my throat, but I didn't look away - couldn't.

I heard a faint buzz then, and one of the men got up sharply. He went into the shop, moving smoothly along what was obviously a well-worn groove; I could even see a faint path worn into the floor.

Something was wrong with one of the men, I realised. His head hung down limply, his shoulders slumped. I'd barely had time to wonder about that when the door opened and three people came through: the assistant, the shopkeeper - and Phil.

I froze.

Phil looked wrong. Blank. His face normally held at least one expression, even at its most relaxed; I'd never seen him so empty before. It took almost no deduction to work out that the shopkeeper - the puppeteer - had done something to him, something to make him like the assistants. The blankness made him look just like the others; featureless, unrecognisable. He was tall and thin like them.

The puppeteer pushed Phil down on a bench and went over to the slumped man. He took his black jacket off him, then his shirt and trousers. Underneath them he wore nothing, except the wires, which were attached directly to his skin, under the skin, digging deep in. The puppeteer unhooked something near the ceiling, then tugged sharply, and the wire slid out of his shoulders. I don't know if it made a noise, and I wouldn't have heard it if it did, but in my imagination it sounded wet, thick and slippery, like pulling a baster from a chicken. I cringed.

The puppeteer picked up the slumped naked man - he was big, but the puppeteer was huge, with muscles standing out all over his body, visible under the black suit - and dropped him in a corner. I think he was dead. I hope so.

The puppeteer grabbed the wires and pulled them over towards Phil. Efficiently, expertly, he stripped him and pushed the wires into his shoulders, deep in and out again so he was firmly attached. The trousers, shirt and jacket were put on him. And then he looked just like the others.

I cried out. Stupidly, like a screaming female sidekick in a thriller, I cried out. But I really couldn't help it. My boyfriend had been turned into a living puppet, and presumably was intended to spend the rest of his so-called life as a zombified shop assistant. It was his fault for being late, I thought wildly; if he'd arrived with me, he'd never have been snatched. As it was, he'd clearly turned up with the right height and weight just when one of the human puppets had finally succumbed to - whatever he had succumbed to. Maybe he'd willed himself to die. I would have.

I thought I was safe for a moment, that I hadn't been heard. But then the back door swung sharply open and the puppeteer grabbed my arm with his awful giant soft fingers in their black gloves.

"Spying," he said with no inflection, pulling me roughly into the back room. "Bad."

"That's my boyfriend!" I screamed, or tried to: I didn't have enough breath in my body to achieve any real volume. "Let him go!"

"No." He released my arms. I stood in the middle of the white room, being stared at by the four automatons, one of whom had woken up in my bed that morning, and watched the puppeteer peel off his gloves. I should have run then, but my legs wouldn't work. Instead I watched his hands emerge, and understood why they'd felt so strange. Each finger was a finger puppet, all tiny black-suited dolls. They lifted up their little heads and their sharp black teeth snapped and chattered at me.

"Go away," said the puppeteer. "Don't come back. Ever." The ten finger puppets came towards me, mouths open. My breath caught. I backed towards the door, whispering, "Please, let him go. Don't torture them like this. Please. How do you think they feel?"

He stopped, and for the first time I saw some kind of expression in his eyes, but I couldn't tell what it was.

"They feel nothing," he said. "And I do not torture them. Do you think I am the puppeteer? I am not the puppeteer." With his fanged fingers, he touched the air above his shoulders. Faintly, running up to the ceiling, I could see razor-sharp, almost-invisible wires coming out of his shoulders.

I opened the back door and ran, and ran, through the rubble-filled yard and the alleyway and the streets of Soho, out of Soho altogether, never to go back.

For all I know, Phil still works there.

~~~~~

Fausterella

She sat in the kitchen, brooding. The dishes were unwashed. The floor was unswept. On the counter lay an envelope, opened, and an engraved invitation, read. It was not for her. It was addressed to Lady Helen, her mistress.

After a while, a large grey mouse emerged from the wainscot, glanced at Fausterella, sighed, climbed into the kitchen sink and started to wash the dishes with its pink tongue. She ignored it.

Upstairs, Lady Helen was plaiting her pale yellow hair into a knot and assessing dresses. Tomorrow night, she knew she would attract the attention of lords, earls and the most ambitious of the nouveau-riche businessmen, but they were of interest only as bait; her sights were set higher. It was true that the Prince was not handsome, and it was also generally conceded that he was perhaps not as well-endowed in the area of talents, good humour and intelligence as might be wished; but he was indisputably Royalty, heir to the throne of the oldest kingdom in Christendom, and as such he must clearly be the shiniest needle in the matrimonial haystack. Lady Helen felt that she deserved the best.

Fausterella also felt that she deserved the best, but it seemed clear that she wasn't going to get it. Instead, she had a dirty kitchen and a mouse.

"Wagner!"

The mouse paused in his work. "What?"

"I want to go to the ball, Wagner," she said, crushing the invitation in a clenched fist. "I'd give anything."

"Why?"

"Why do you think? So that I can meet, and then at a later date marry, the Prince."

Wagner raised an eyebrow. "Are you sure? I hear he's a little dull. And mainly interested in fox hunting and beating up his servants."

"As if that matters," she snapped. "His wife will be a princess, and never lift a finger. No more toiling my life away down here." The mouse glanced pointedly at the fork he'd been washing. Fausterella shrugged. "Look, I'm beautiful; you know I am." (I'm a mouse, muttered Wagner, you all look alike to me; but she didn't hear.) "Once he sees me, if I'm cleaned up and dressed up, I know I can get him." She had some basis for this belief. Several of the local men had already proposed to her, some repeatedly, but as they were all working class they had been rejected without ceremony. Or politeness.

"So steal one of her ladyship's dresses and go to the ball," suggested the mouse.

"Maybe I will," she mused. "Once she's out of the house tomorrow night, I could do whatever I wanted. But then how do I get there, and what do I use for an invitation? Oh, it's too *hard*."

The girl flung herself down on a cushion. Wagner continued to wash up, reflecting that if she was hoping him to come up with a miraculous solution to her problems, she had overestimated both his abilities and his desire to help her. Nevertheless, due to their long association and proximity, he had a certain sardonic affection for the kitchen maid, and found himself vaguely wishing that someone would appear to make her wish come true. He was therefore pleased, if startled, when he turned round and discovered that a being had appeared in the corner of the kitchen.

"Hello," said the being.

Fausterella jumped.

The being sat down on a kitchen chair. Its features were androgynous, its appearance indeterminate, and its most noticeable aspect was the large red tail wrapped around its gauzy body. The tail flicked towards Fausterella.

"I'm here," said the thing, "in the aspect of your fairy godmother. I believe you are in need of one?"

Fausterella nodded, breathless.

"Then pray consider me the answer to your prayers. My only desire is to make your dreams come true. What do you dream of?"

"Money, power and being a princess," said the girl in a rush of words. "I know it sounds shallow, but you try living in a kitchen."

"Believe me," said her red-tailed fairy godmother, "I have no intention of judging you. In fact, I'm pleased. Fulfilling your needs should be easy, a lovely girl like you. Let me guess, you want to go to the ball tomorrow, there to catch your prince in the snare of your doubtless enchanting beauty?"

"Yes!"

"Very well." The godmother made a complicated tail-based movement and a red folder appeared in its hand. "In here is an invitation to the ball, a voucher for a reputable taxi service to get you there and back, and enough money to provide you with clothing and accessories." It handed the folder to Fausterella.

"Thank you!" She bounced a little and made a movement towards hugging the godmother, but decided against it; the tail looked rather sharp around the edges. "How can I ever repay you?"

"Interesting you should mention that." The being made another complicated movement; a document appeared. "I just need you to sign this. It's a-"

Before it had a chance to finish the sentence, Fausterella seized a pen and wrote her name in sprawling capitals at the bottom of the page. "There," she said. "Now, if you don't mind, I've got dresses to plan."

The godmother shrugged. "Fair enough." It tucked the piece of paper carefully away. "If you marry the prince," ("If!" scoffed the girl,) "this will come into effect. I'll see you at the wedding.

"Oh," it added casually, "to start off your outfit, have these." On the floor in front of the stove there was suddenly a pair of high-heeled, strappy, velvety, bright red shoes in Fausterella's exact size. She gazed at them, entranced. "Wear them to the ball and the prince will certainly propose."

And with that the being vanished, leaving only a trace of rainbow-slick oil on the floor.

For the next twenty-four hours, Fausterella whirled. She sneaked out (leaving Wagner to make lunch for Lady Helen) and bought a dress of blood-red satin, clingy and low-cut. She bought garnets for her neck and ears and a crimson headdress. When she tried them all on, that evening, the contrast with her long black hair and dark skin was vivid and stunning. Even Wagner stared.

"Am I going to get him?" She twirled; the dress flared; the shoes glinted.

"I really think you are," he said.

It all went according to plan.

The taxi deposited her at the steps of the palace and even the footmen couldn't take their eyes off her. She glided into the ballroom snakelike, ravishing, and the Prince, who had just been contemplating asking Lady Helen to dance for a second time, instead dropped his glass and stepped forwards into the shards to take Fausterella into his arms. In her high red shoes, she found she was almost as tall as he was.

She smiled; she danced; she agreed with everything he said, and she tossed her black hair until it looked like the foamy wave on a midnight sea. He proposed halfway through the second dance. Fausterella smiled a triumphant yes and the announcement was made at midnight. They stood side by side at the top of the stairs and the guests applauded.

Most of the unmarried women did not clap with any enthusiasm, with the exception of Lady Helen. During her dance with the prince she had found him much as rumour had predicted: loutish, boring and prone to long anecdotes about the iniquities of various footmen he had found fault with. Despite Fausterella's views on the subject, Lady Helen was not a bad woman at heart, and had no desire to become a princess if the price was a lifetime of listening to servants being hit around the head. She was therefore genuinely indifferent to the prince's sudden engagement, at least until she recognised her kitchen maid as the future princess. Even then, she thought she must have been mistaken till she heard the name.

"Fausterella?" She pushed her way forwards through the crowd and stared. "Hey! That's my maid!"

Fausterella flushed a crimson to match her outfit. "How dare you!" she shouted. "That woman is jealous! Arrest her for spreading lies!"

"Guards!" cried the prince. Lady Helen was picked up bodily and carried away, too shocked to say anything further. Fausterella smiled at her retreating back.

She knew she couldn't go back to the house anyway; she had insinuated to the prince that she was a foreigner of mysterious but aristocratic background, driven from her country by the violence of an evil stepmother. So she abandoned the kitchen and her belongings, and Wagner, without a second thought, and moved into the palace until the wedding day. The prince bought her roomfuls of dresses, knickers, stockings, jewellery and shoes, and sometimes at night she gathered some of her new clothes together and rolled on them, delirious with acquisitive joy. She found her fiancé almost unbearable as a companion, but that was of minor importance; and in the spirit of being interested in his hobbies, she took up being abusive to her maids. It was intoxicating to have the power to insult without consequences, and the prince loved her all the more for it.

A few days before the wedding, it occurred to Fausterella to ask what had become of Lady Helen. It turned out that she was still in a palace dungeon; the kingdom was not one that bothered much with trials or the operations of justice. As a wedding present, Fausterella asked the prince if he would give her Lady Helen as a maid.

"Of course, my love," he said. He immediately stripped Lady Helen of her title, confiscated her house, and had her delivered to his bride-to-be dressed in specially-distressed rags. Fausterella clapped her hands.

"This is a morality tale," she said to Helen. "The meek shall inherit the earth and the proud shall be humbled."

"But you were never meek, and I wasn't especially proud," said her new maid, who had not yet adjusted to the realities of her position. "And both of us were merely living out the roles assigned to us by society. Anyway, I gave you every other Sunday off and never complained about your terrible cooking. Did I deserve several weeks in a dungeon for telling the truth?"

Fausterella slapped her. "Sort out my clothes, and stop talking." Helen's eyes dropped. She picked up an armful of dresses and moved away.

The evening before the wedding, there was a scratching at Fausterella's door. She opened it, snapping: "I told you, not before the wedding night!" But the noise was from lower down.

"Wagner?"

"Hello," said the mouse. Fausterella found herself unexpectedly pleased to see him; she even picked him up and hugged him. Wagner politely disentangled himself and climbed onto her bed.

The almost-princess experienced the unfamiliar sensation of guilt. "Look, I'm sorry I didn't come back to say goodbye. Everything happened so fast and I couldn't let him know who I really was…"

"It's fine, it's fine. I'm pleased for you." Wagner appraised the rich furnishings of her bedroom and lifted an mousy eyebrow, impressed. "That's not why I'm here. Listen. You remember that contract you signed for your fairy godmother?"

"Yes," she said vaguely; actually, she had almost forgotten it.

"I was tidying the kitchen and found a copy had been left for you, in a drawer. Don't you want to know what you signed up to?"

"I suppose." Wagner unfolded the piece of paper he'd been carrying. Fausterella skimmed it, and blanched.

"Wagner!"

"I know."

She read it again.

"My soul?"

"So it seems."

"Why does my fairy godmother want my soul?"

"I think we have to accept that the thing that appeared to us was rather more, or less, than a fairy godmother."

"What shall I do? I don't want to die on my wedding day! Or at all!"

"There may be a way out." He tapped the paper with a claw. "Read it again."

She did.

The next morning, Helen dressed Fausterella in gleaming white from head to ankle, ready for her wedding. The bride insisted, however, on wearing red shoes. Her maid asked no questions. The shoes were in any case hidden by the length of the dress.

"Stay by me," Fausterella instructed Helen.

As she walked through the silent, awestruck crowd, towards the prince and the priest, the very-nearly-princess found that she was not at all intimidated by her new position. She had always known she was born for this. From the look in the prince's eyes, he saw it too. They repeated the phrases of love and loyalty to each other and their eyes shone with somewhat different – but similarly joyful - emotions. The prince was marrying the woman he loved. Fausterella was marrying lifelong wealth. They were both about equally happy.

As soon as the vows were finished and the priest had proclaimed the couple prince and princess, there was a shimmering noise at the back of the palace chapel and the red-tailed fairy godmother appeared. It caught Fausterella's eye and waved its copy of the contract meaningfully. She nodded.

"Excuse me a minute," she said to the prince.

"I'm sorry?" The guests stared.

"I'll be back. We're finished with the formalities, aren't we?"

"I suppose so…" The prince waved a hand at the guests and they started to disperse, confused and chatting. Fausterella hurried to the back.

"Princess Fausterella." The godmother bowed. "Congratulations."

"Thank you."

"But you should have read your contract before you so eagerly put your signature to it. At midnight on your wedding night, I am bound to tell you that the owner of those red shoes will find her soul belongs to me."

"Oh, I read the contract," she said, calm. "But I think you'll find there's something of a loophole in your wording." She gestured to Helen, who was watching the proceedings from a safe but intrigued distance. "This is my new maid. She's been very useful and I think she deserves a present. Helen!"

"Yes, your highness?"

"Here – as a memento of my wedding, I give you my shoes."
The new princess bent to remove them, frowned, pulled at one
foot, pulled at the other foot, sat on the ground and pulled at
her shoes until she gasped. (The wedding guests, eating
canapés on the other side of the room, were open-mouthed.)

The godmother watched with the patience of someone who has
seen this scene before.

"They won't come off!" screamed Fausterella, stating the
obvious.

"Of course not," said her godmother. "Do you think I'm so
easily fooled? I'll see you at midnight, then." It grinned,
shimmered, and vanished.

Fausterella glared at Helen and at Wagner, who was sitting on
a cornice and eating a piece of popcorn he'd found. "Help
me!"

"Your highness," said Helen, slightly hysterically, "from what
I can gather, you've just tried to trick me into losing my soul,
on top of having me imprisoned. I really don't think I can help
you any further."

"And I've already done as much as I can, to be honest," said
Wagner, tossing a popcorn kernel on to the stone floor.

"But there's nobody else!"

"There's the prince," said Wagner, nodding in his direction.
"Your life partner, your lord and master. The one over there,
trying to retie his tie and failing." Fausterella glanced towards
her new husband and wondered for just a moment whether
death might be preferable to a life with him; but practicality
quickly reasserted itself.

"I'll think of something," she said.

At midnight, she lay in the royal bed, shoes still firmly affixed, the prince blissfully asleep some distance away from her. (It was a very wide bed.) The godmother appeared on the headboard. It seemed larger now; its tail was definitely forked and it glistened like a sword, or rather two conjoined swords.

"Don't kill me," said the princess in an urgent whisper, sitting up. "What will you accept in place of my death? Sex? Money? The death of someone I love?"

"No, no and who? My dear, there's nobody you love." Fausterella had to admit the truth of this.

"But the death of someone who loves you – who knows you, accepts you and still loves you - that's a different matter."

"Really?"

"Really."

Fausterella considered. Only one name came to mind.

"Wagner?" she offered.

The godmother grinned. "Yes. In his own way he loves you. You'd swap Wagner's life for yours?"

"I would," she said without hesitation.

"Thank you."

Her face lit up. "It's that easy?"

"Yes," it said. Her shoes loosened and fell off. "Losing your soul is that easy. Thank you." Its tail curled around something dark and glowing. Fausterella felt a sensation that was not quite pain, not quite chill; a sense that she had lost something but would never remember exactly what. "I never said you would die," it added. "I wish you a long and happy, for some value of happy, life."

And for the last time, it vanished.

Not Just for Christmas

I hate living alone.

I particularly hate waking up in the middle of the night in an empty house and realising I'm hungry. And I hate shuffling with half-closed eyes down the stairs to the kitchen, leaving the lights off in case they wake me up. I suppose I should leave a Mars bar by my bed to avoid having to do all this, but I never remember. So I woke up in the middle of the night, in my empty house, one night towards the end of June, and I shuffled downstairs to find chocolate.

Of course, on this occasion, the house wasn't actually empty.

I opened the fridge, squinting as the light came on, and fumbled around for the Twix I was sure lived in there somewhere. I found it, ate it in two practised bites, closed the door, began shuffling back through the kitchen, and became aware that the French windows were silhouetting something. Someone. A man, dressed in a smart black suit, was standing outside my kitchen.

Then, exactly one second later, a man in a smart black suit was standing inside my kitchen. The crash of the windows breaking echoed as I watched him stagger towards me. *He's ill*, I thought. Then I thought, *He's insane*. And then he moaned and his blind eyes started at me and his dead arms reached for me, and I knew what he was.

Now very wide awake, I took several short steps backwards. He followed. Could I stab him with a kitchen knife, I thought wildly? No, I answered wildly, they didn't die from that - they didn't die at all. I'd have to trap him somewhere. Where? The cellar, obviously. Right. I backed quickly into the correct corner of the kitchen and lifted the trapdoor. They weren't supposed to be that bright, were they? And indeed he wasn't. He lumbered over to me, moaning, and fell headfirst into the darkness. A muffled moan indicated that he had hit the ground, or probably the pile of coal.

I locked the trapdoor and retreated upstairs to think.

I didn't think I'd slept at all, but it had become morning without my noticing. I opened my eyes, thanked God it was a Saturday, and decided to stay in bed for a while in order to contemplate my options. The thing was, I wasn't scared. There was a zombie in my cellar, and what had been my first thought on waking up? *I'm not alone in the house any more*, I'd thought, sleepily and contentedly. I had company.

I'd always wanted a pet.

The trapdoor creaked quietly as I opened it. I peered down, bracing myself to slam the door shut on Maxwell's head. (I'd decided to call him Maxwell. It had been the name of my hamster as a child. I'd been very fond of that hamster. I wish I'd remembered to feed him.) But the zombie didn't leap at me. When my eyes adjusted, I saw him sitting in a corner, slumped. Had he been sleeping? I really had to learn more about his care and feeding.

Feeding. Hmm. I pushed the thought aside for a moment and said, "Maxwell?" in a bright voice.

He looked up. He was freshly dead, not rotted at all; perfect. He was even slightly handsome, dark-haired and dark-eyed, although I do restrict my love interests to the living. He didn't frighten me. In an odd way, he made me feel safe, even powerful. After all, he was the one in the cellar.

"You wait there," I said, and closed the trapdoor. I wandered into the living room, pensive.

I owned my house; my parents had left it to me when they died, and I was an only child. It was far too big for me, but I didn't want to sell it; it was my home. I didn't tend to invite people over much, and I had no relatives I was close to. I was ideally placed to look after a pet zombie, I decided. He could stay in the cellar. Zombies didn't need exercise.

But did they need feeding?

Only one way to find out. I'd keep him for a bit and see how it went. Maybe zombies didn't need to feed. Maybe they just liked the taste. It was worth a try.

I settled into a routine. Every morning before work I'd open the trapdoor and chat to Maxwell. I liked the way he didn't ask me why I was still single, or try to drunkenly chat me up, or tell me I needed to lose weight. His conversational style was intensely relaxing. I'd talk, and he'd listen. His sightless eyes would stare at me, and occasionally he would moan softly in what I took to be agreement. I poured out all my troubles, my ex-boyfriends, my bullying managers, and he just... listened. It was blissful.

After a week or so, however, I had to admit that my plan wasn't going to work quite as I wanted it to. There was a distinct smell rising from my basement, and bits of Maxwell were starting to drop off. The lack of food was getting to him. One morning I came down to find his leg had fallen off. I thought about trying to glue it back on, but I wasn't sure I had any glue. So I apologised to my zombie and explained that he was just going to have to do without that leg. It had crawled off into the corner, anyway, and was twitching slightly.

I was going to have to feed him. Or, to put it in the harsh terms I'd been avoiding, I was going to have to find him some brains.

There were tests I could make, though. Maybe I wouldn't have to actually, you know, kill anyone. First I tried him with shop-bought calves' brains. No good. He tried, I could see, but he just couldn't choke them down. So next, I got very drunk and raided a local graveyard for a body. I found one that had been alive only days earlier, but even so, he wouldn't take it.

It was starting to feel like catering for a fussy toddler. I briefly wondered about trying to feed him his own leg, but decided it might not go down well. As it were.

The only option that remained was to invite someone over who I really, really disliked.

James Grant was a successful middle manager who lived across the road from me. At the recent New Year's Eve party of a mutual friend and neighbour, he had attempted to grope me on top of a pile of coats. Admittedly he had been drunk and I'd fought him off using only one hand, but nevertheless, he was an obvious candidate for pet food. Plus, if I invited him to my house, he would definitely come, and because he lived alone, he wouldn't tell anyone where he was going. I waited till Saturday afternoon and dropped a note through his letterbox asking if he wanted to drop by for a drink at 10pm. He did.

I hadn't quite worked out how I'd manage it, but in the end it was easy, really. Thus:

Me: "James darling, before I get your drink, I must show you what I've got in the cellar. You'll be amazed."

Him: "Really? How fascinating. You really are a very fascinating woma-" He leant in, I pushed from behind,

Maxwell roared enthusiastically, and I quickly shut the trapdoor before I had to see what happened next.

An hour or so later, I looked in on Maxwell and found him looking much healthier. Whatever the zombie equivalent of a glossy coat and wet nose is, he had it. Even his dismembered leg looked more cheerful. James's body lay forlornly to one side, looking much the same except for the missing top of his head.

But there was something I'd failed to take into account. When I opened the trapdoor on Sunday morning, I had two zombies. James had risen and was moaning enthusiastically along with Maxwell.

Oops.

And now I had to feed them both.

Three weeks later, I knew I was in well over my head. I'd started running out of people I disliked, and there were now fifteen zombies living in the cellar. I lived in daily terror of the police visiting me, and I was starting to think that living alone hadn't been that bad after all. The constant moaning was keeping me awake at night, and the cellar was overcrowded. A Health and Safety visitor would definitely have banned me from ever keeping pets again. I stood looking down at the shambling, shuffling mass of brain-eating undead people in my basement and I had to ask myself, was a zombie for life, or just for Christmas?

I knew what my answer was. So I began to make a list of things I could do with them.

It went as follows:

1. Employ them as street sweepers. Pro: they can probably manage to sweep. Con: the streets would probably end up dirtier than before.

2. Join them up with an escort agency. Pro: there's got to be someone with a zombie fetish out there. Con: there are lot of people who don't have one and would sue me.

3. Assistants to brain surgeons. Pro: useful for getting rid of bits of brain that would otherwise be thrown away. Con: liable to eat rest of brain as well.

At this point I remembered that all these options had the massive downside that I'd have to explain where I'd got fifteen zombies from. So I couldn't employ them. I couldn't kill them. I was stuck with them.

But could I *sell* them? Or if not them, at least their surroundings?

Yes, I thought, I could. I put the house up for sale.

It worked brilliantly. I ensured my pets were well fed to reduce the smell, and placed pot-pourri in strategic locations to cover any residue. I put a rug over the trapdoor and simply claimed the house didn't have a cellar. Nobody noticed. I told the estate agents to put the house on the market for £10,000 less than they thought it was worth, and within a week, I had three offers. I took the highest one. The buyers were a middle-aged couple who worked in land management. They had no children. I don't think I could have sold the place to people who had children. That would have been unethical.

The money bought me a plane ticket and a small flat in a small town in Argentina. It's nice here. I'm learning Spanish. And as long as I never go back, I'll never have to know what happened to my zombies. I avoid the newspapers, too. It's peaceful here.

I still hate living alone, though. I miss Maxwell. And sometimes in the middle of the night, I wake up and lie in my bed, in the heat, thinking of maybe visiting the quiet cemetery down the road, seeing if I could hear any moaning. Finding myself a new pet. But I know I mustn't, and I don't do it. I probably never will.

Probably.

~~~~~

The Kick Inside

It had been years and years, I realised, since Jonathan and I had last driven though the Yorkshire Dales. When we used to live in Leeds, we'd come up here almost every weekend with a couple of friends and get stoned sitting on a hilltop somewhere, gazing across the fields and having random, poetic conversations. But we'd moved down south, and soon after that we'd lost touch with our Yorkshire friends, and somehow we didn't get back up this way very often. This weekend was a treat, a celebration; also a reminder of what London lacked in terms of landscape, much as I loved the city.

I rolled down the car window and tried to memorise the view. The moor rolled away from us, a huge patchwork quilt in shades of dark, pale and emerald green, stitched with hedges, knotted with gnarly trees. But the metaphor was too domestic, really. Quilts were cosy and the moor wasn't cosy, it was a controlled wildness, somewhere you could get lost in and perhaps never be found.

I could have taken a photo instead of trying to imprint the landscape on my mind, but we were driving at sixty miles an hour: part of Jonathan's love for the moor was the sensation of driving fast through the hilly, twisted roads, almost empty of traffic. So I just stared in a relaxed sort of way. As always, the Dales looked virtually uninhabited. There were farmhouses visible in the middle of fields, and we passed through a few tiny villages – six houses and a church, maybe a pub if you were lucky – but we hadn't seen any actual people so far this afternoon. It was a hot early-summer day, so they were probably all asleep somewhere. The thought reminded me that I could do with a short nap myself. I clicked the car seat back as far as it would go, and fumbled round the side pocket till I found some music that would fit the landscape. I ended up with Kate Bush's The Kick Inside. Her voice gave the moor a suitably sinister quality.

"There's room for a life in your womb, woman. Inside of you can be two, woman..."

I lay back, smiled to myself and stroked my stomach, which was getting rounder every day. Jonathan glanced over and smiled too. "Baby kicking yet?"

"Not yet. Give it time."

"It's had plenty of time. Want it to kick now."

"Well, you tell it then. It's not listening to me."

"By the way, do you have any preference as to where we go?"

"Random driving's fine with me. Find somewhere interesting."

"Cool." The car whooshed down a steep incline and Jonathan made a 'wheee!' noise to go with it, a habit I found very endearing. "I'm going to turn left at the next junction and see where that takes us."

"OK. I'm going to doze for a bit."

"You'll miss the countryside."

"I can't help it, I need to sleep. It's hard work being pregnant."

"So you claim. I have my doubts."

"I can't be bothered to hit you. Consider yourself beaten up, ok?" Jonathan groaned theatrically, then went back to making 'wheee!' noises as the car swirled round bends and down slopes. I closed my eyes and pulled my sunhat over my face.

I woke up about half an hour later to find that we were surrounded by trees. A sign by the side of the road read: 'Woodlands open to the public by kind permission of the Earl of Swinton'.

"Where are we?" I said groggily.

"In the Earl of Swinton's woods, apparently. I just followed some random turnings. Shall we have a look?"

"Sure, why not?" The trees by the road were sparse, but as we drove the woods got thicker until all we could see was sunlight glinting through branches. The sun was starting to give me a headache. The Kate Bush album had stopped while I'd been asleep; I started to search for more music but couldn't be bothered to rummage, so we watched the dense woods closing around us in silence.

"Want to have a look round?"

"I don't think I have the energy. You go."

We found a clearing to our right and Jonathan parked us in the shade under a spreading tree. "Are you sure you don't want to come for a walk? Might do you good."

"Seriously, I can barely sit up. I'm going to sleep a bit more." I yawned.

"OK."

I lay back again, feeling guilty that I wasn't up to joining Jonathan. But my lethargy was all-consuming, and soon I was asleep again, one hand wrapped protectively round my abdomen in a gesture that had become habitual since I'd first found out I was pregnant.

I came back to consciousness when the car door opened. "You should have come," said my husband excitedly. "It's really cool. I went quite deep into the woods and I found a ring of standing stones. I don't know if they're ancient or recent, but someone's been using them – there were fires lit inside the circle. And behind the stones there's a shallow cave with a kind of stone altar inside it. I sat there for a while. The whole place is deserted. I almost felt I was intruding."

"Wow." I was genuinely impressed. It's rare for Jonathan to get excited about things. "How bizarre that you drove through some random countryside and found all that."

"Isn't it?" He started the car. "I wish you could have seen it. It's very peaceful. Well, maybe a little creepy, but peaceful as well."

"It does sound a little creepy," I said sleepily. I pulled the car seat back to upright, feeling that I'd missed enough of the afternoon. But when I looked out of the window, the first thing I saw was a dead pheasant by the side of the road. We passed it quickly, so I didn't have a chance to check my initial impression that there was something odd about it. But then a minute later we passed a dead rabbit. "Can you slow down a bit?" I said.

"Why?"

"There's something odd about all the roadkill."

Jonathan glanced out the window. "You mean how they look kind of stretched?"

"Yes!" I said, startled. "And there's something weird about their legs, too."

"I noticed that on the way here. There's loads of dead animals round this area. I wouldn't worry about the oddness – animals get run over, they're going to change shape a bit."

"Yeah, I suppose so." I knew he was right, but nevertheless I kept an eye out. We passed dead mice, voles, birds, more pheasants, more rabbits, all looking somehow different, mutated, at least to my eyes. Occasionally we braked to avoid live animals; they moved quickly, but even so I couldn't shake the impression that they looked wrong, too. There was something about the way they ran that made me uneasy. I found myself hoping that we didn't come across any people.

"Did you say somebody had been using the standing stones?" I thought aloud.

"Looked like it, yes. Someone had been lighting fires, anyway. And there was some stuff, rubbish, scattered round the stones."

"What kind of stuff?"

"Oh, just… stuff." It was easy enough to tell when Jonathan didn't want to talk about something. Usually that wouldn't stop me, but this time I decided to let it go.

Well, more or less. "Were there any dead animals inside the circle?"

"Well, yes," he said reluctantly. "A couple."

"Did you look at them? Did they look normal?"

"I didn't look at them closely, no." He made a face. "I wasn't that keen to, to be honest. I don't have your ghoulish curiosity."

"Just wondering."

I had the urge to put on some very, very frivolous music. Sixties pop, something like that, something bubbly. But I didn't. I sat quietly, waiting for us to get clear of the close woods, away from the corpses littering our road, and back to our comfortable, safe hotel. I didn't like the trees any more. I didn't want to see any more elongated, legless mammals in the corner of my vision.

"One thing," Jonathan said suddenly, as if he'd decided to be more honest than he really wanted to be. "The largest stone in the circle, it was odd, it had a snake figure carved into it. Must have taken ages. There was a dead snake on the stone altar, too."

"Odd," I said quietly. My desire not to see any of the people who lived round here was becoming a state of nervous anxiety. But we didn't see anyone. We left the woods and came out onto the open dales. I breathed deeply, glad that I hadn't gone to see what was in those woods. Beside me, Jonathan was quiet. There was tension in his muscles.

My hand was on my stomach. As we drove out of the Swinton woods, I felt the sensation that I'd been looking forward to for months. Inside me, the baby moved

But it wasn't a kick.

~~~~~

Stepmother

She was thirty and I fifteen, when we met. (Now I am thirty and, somewhere, she is forty-five; I wonder if she looks it.)

She was a small woman, and graceful, with dark hair curling under her chin and skin the colour of her hair. You could hear her wherever she was in the house, because she sang quietly to herself as she wandered around, though I could never catch the song and she never knew she was doing it. Her mouth was wide, her fingers and toes long.

Fifteen years old, and I had never felt anything before like the jolt as my father led in his new wife, my new stepmother, with an air of possession for which I could have killed him. She looked across at me — we were the same height then; I am taller now — and smiled, as one smiles at one's husband's daughter who is a stranger. I did not smile back. I blinked, stumbled and reached out for the hand she offered without taking my eyes off her face, so that I missed it completely and my fingers closed over air.

My father looked at me, puzzled. "Ella, this is your new mother. I hope you will accept her as part of the household, and her two girls. They are younger than you, and are eager to make friends."

"Of course, father." I wondered if I would be able to get out of the room without falling over. "May I go now?"

He looked disappointed, but nodded. As I left I heard him explaining to her that I was a nervous girl, who had spent much time alone. He was sure having a bigger family would be beneficial to me.

I no longer remember exactly how I felt that evening, curled up in my velvet and oak room, listening to the quiet noise of conversation downstairs, knowing that I had fallen in love with my own stepmother. I know, though, that I felt tainted; there was a sense of loss, possibly a loss of innocence, certainly a loss of childhood. Some relationships are so strange as to be virtually inconceivable, and to allow oneself to conceive of them is to enter a new, unsettling world. I knew that had a secret I would have to keep forever; the alternative was public shame. Not to mention the risk of her revulsion, which was less a risk than a certainty.

When my thoughts had reached this point, I realised there was only one means of keeping this unnatural thing from them all, one part I could play convincingly. I would have to cast her as the evil stepmother, and I would have to believe it myself, at least in part. I would have to hate her, in order to stop myself loving her.

Two years passed, and then my father died.

He died believing that I hated my stepmother. I even pretended to loathe her two daughters, though I found it difficult to repress my pity for them—they were shy misshapen creatures who spent their time frantically dressing up and putting make-up on each other in an effort to disguise their looks. Sometimes I crept into their bedroom and replaced the unbecoming clothes with prettier dresses; they had no taste in dress.

That was not my only nocturnal excursion.

After I had recovered from my initial grief for my father — for I had loved him, though never as intensely as I had envied him — I became aware that she now slept alone. A few days later I found myself floating up the stairs towards her bedroom, pretending to be helplessly sleepwalking. I drifted into her room, deliberately only half-aware of what I was doing, and slowed for a moment to find the shape of her sleeping body under the thin sheet; it was a hot night. I leaned towards her and ran a finger, every nerve ending alert, over her dark outflung arm. She did not wake. I knelt by the bed for perhaps twenty minutes. She did not wake. Finally I stood up and, clasping my arms tightly about myself, went back downstairs.

After that I knew I couldn't trust myself anywhere near her. I told her that my hatred for her and her daughters was so great that I did not want to belong to the same family as them. I would dress myself in rags and be their servant, live in the kitchen and sweep their dirt. She remonstrated with me, being a kind woman who had tried tirelessly to win my affection, but I would not listen. I put on my oldest dress and went down to the cellar, vowing never to come up again.

A few months later came the ball invitation. She came downstairs, obviously nervous but determined, and showed me the embossed card. It shone luminously in the kitchen's darkness and dirtiness.

"Please come to the ball, Ella. This is no way for a seventeen-year-old girl to live. Come up from the cellar, put on a pretty gown and perhaps you'll get to meet the prince." Her voice sounded like creamed chocolate. Tears came to my eyes every time I heard it.

"I can't," I said hopelessly, too exhausted to swear at her as was my normal practice. "I can't."

"I'll find you a dress. I'll hire us a carriage, I'll buy you slippers. I just want you to be happy, Ella. We could be a proper family."

"I can never be part of your family." In the dark I half-saw her eyes lower, her mouth drop sadly; she genuinely believed I hated her. She sighed, let the card fall and walked away.

For two days I lived in the kitchen, mainly curled up in the corner staring at nothing. The third evening, I woke from a shallow nap and realised that it was the evening of the ball. There was a small commotion going on under the table: the mice who cohabited with me in my self-imposed prison were tearing something up with their tiny gleaming teeth. The thing they were tearing gleamed too. It was a card. I rescued it from the mice and brushed off the dust; still usable, I thought. And my room upstairs still held my clothes and shoes. Why not?

A bath and a change of clothes later, I was gazing into my mirror with delight. There are few troubles that a seventeen-year-old girl cannot mitigate with pretty dresses, and I had chosen my prettiest. White silk, strapless, falling to my ankles, accentuating my curves and emphasising my height. I added transparent sandals and a dark green velvet shawl, and set off to the palace.

It was good to see people again, and I suddenly became aware how much I had lost in my two years of miserable incarceration. Friends and distant relations rushed up to me, asking where on earth I had got to. I smiled mysteriously, having no answer ready, and floated down the stairs to the great hall where the prince was dancing.

I saw her at once. She was wearing a crimson ball gown the colour of blood; my heart's blood of course, I thought, almost falling down the stairs because again I could not stop looking at her face. It was a troubled face. I wanted to take away the trouble but I knew I was its cause, so instead I turned to the man beside me and accepted his invitation to dance. It was the prince, as it turned out. I had known him for years, and he was usually a relaxing companion. Tonight, however, he seemed unable to talk about anything but my beauty, and my attention kept wandering. I wanted to make sure she did not see me, and I knew I had to leave before she and her daughters did, so they would not know I had left the house. The clock struck midnight.

The prince was still telling me how wonderful I looked, but I shook him off and ran towards the stairs, losing my shawl and a slipper in the process but grateful that I had managed to escape without her seeing me. I wasn't even sure why I had come, except that I had to see her again.

With bleeding feet—I had taken off the other slipper in order to run faster—I made it to the kitchen in time, and hung up my white dress behind the door where it would not be noticed. I heard them return, laughing and talking; apparently one of the daughters had made a hit with a duke.

The next day, I resumed my duties, wondering how if I really intended to spend the rest of my life in a locked kitchen. My stepmother had given up on me; now she sent one of her daughters downstairs when she needed to tell me something.

So it was that the eldest of them came running downstairs three days after the ball, breathless with excitement and terror. The terror was of me, for I was an object of fear to them. The excitement, it transpired, was because the prince was upstairs, asking for me and saying that he had something of mine to return.

I slipped on the white dress and came upstairs, deciding I could manage to see an old friend and assuming my stepmother would be staying out of the way. But no, she was chatting with the prince in the drawing room, and did not leave when she saw me.

"Ella, his highness wishes to return your shawl," she said, not looking at me.

"Didn't you find my slipper as well?" I asked him, as the shoes were considerably more expensive.

"Just the shawl, I'm afraid. I did want to ask you something, though."

"Yes?"

He exchanged a glance with my stepmother. "I know you've had some, well, problems, but we've known each other a long time and I find you very attractive and I need a princess—"

"You want to marry me?" He had a bit of a stammer and I couldn't be bothered to wait for the end of the sentence; it was obvious what it was going to be.

"Well, yes."

I shrugged. "OK."

He threw himself at my feet. "My lady! I swear I will make you the happiest woman in the world!"

"Well, actually," I said, "there is something you can do for me. You see this woman?"

She looked at me apprehensively. I looked back, for once allowing myself to gaze as much as I wanted. I could not marry the prince knowing she was still there, living in the city, not loving me, not desiring me. I could not even look at her any more. I had to make sure she was not there, that she was absent from my life.

"She locked me in the cellar and fed me scraps." I said venomously, tremblingly. "She let the mice nibble my clothes, and she tried to prevent me going to the ball," I allowed a carefully balanced touch of anger and sadness to underlay my confessional tone. "I will only be happy if she is punished. I cannot marry you unless I am happy."

We both stared at my stepmother with loathing, and she saw her fate in our eyes.

"Do you have a pocket knife?"

He did.

I opened it up and he held her for me while I slashed her face, once on each cheek. Something inside me loosened and collapsed. She did not scream or say anything, but she cried, and that was enough.

"Shall I kill her?" he said, meeting my eyes with fear and submission.

"No. But she must be imprisoned, to stop her being wicked to others," I said decisively. "Her children can live with relations. Far away," I added, to make sure they were not a nuisance, or a reminder, to me.

"Anything you say, my darling." There was submission and fear in his eyes, but something else as well, perhaps a loss of illusion? Maybe it was the sight of the blood splashing onto my face and gown.

Thirteen years ago, it was. Now I am thirty, and she will be forty-five in her dungeon, with healed but visible scars on her face, her skin less creamy smooth now, I expect, her eyes older and far more tired. And I am a princess, rich and beautiful and powerful. The prince is afraid of me and of my temper, and my recurring mental problems, and my knife. So I rule the kingdom, for he dares not refuse me anything.

Also, he still hopes that, one day, I will allow him to touch me.

~~~~~

The Winter Tree
A Seasonal Tragedy

The village of Muddlenose was extremely tiny and extremely isolated, and was situated not quite in the heart of England but perhaps somewhere around its stomach, or small intestine. Few people ever found it or even looked for it. Indeed, any signs pointing the way to Muddlenose tended to blow down in the wind or be unexpectedly burnt to a crisp one night, such was the Muddlenosians' desire for privacy. And the villagers got on well enough by themselves, mostly: marrying each other and giving birth to small Muddlenosians, each emerging from the womb with the village's characteristic expression of suspicious self-sufficiency.

"We don't need anyone else," Mrs Mallowfudge would often say to her gentleman visitor, Audacious Skinwillow. And he would reply, "And they don't need us." Or sometimes, "And we don't *want* anyone else, either." Then they would nod firmly at each other before indulging in self-sufficient, Muddlenosian lovemaking. For the village was not opposed to fornication between the unmarried, or indeed adultery (for it was never clear if there was or had ever been a Mr Mallowfudge). In fact, the village was rarely opposed to anything, provided it was done by a Muddlenosian.

One year, however, in spite of their precautions, a stranger did find Muddlenose. He stumbled in one day in high summer, blinking as if he had just emerged from darkness, and somehow he stayed.

The woman from whom he rented a room, Miss Audrey Chasepaper (a lady of indeterminate age, weight and moral fibre), could not pronounce his name. So he came to be called Mr Glittergrime. Once he had arranged terms with Miss

Chasepaper, Mr Glittergrime was rarely heard to speak. He stayed in his room, or went walking in the extensive woods to the east of the village, and seemed content. The villagers began to ignore his tall, spare figure as it hurried about the market square or disappeared among the trees, and before long Muddlenose had more or less accepted him.

Until winter came.

Autumn was long that year and winter came suddenly, breaking in on the brown and gold landscape almost overnight, like a guest who hopes to distract from his lateness with the violence of his entry. In other words, one morning there was a chill in the air; the next day there was a shimmering of frost; and on the third day, the village woke up to find itself deep in snow.

But not the snow they expected. For the snowfall was not, as they had previously found it to be, white. It was black. Black snowflakes fell and covered the square, plastered the thatches of houses, and shrouded the old oak tree by the village church. On the roads and paths, tremendous black snowdrifts made passage difficult. The snow was thick and deep and beautiful, but the villagers of Muddlenose did not notice that. They simply stared in astonishment at the midnight blackness all around them, for they had no idea what to think.

"What's going on?" said Mrs Mallowfudge to Audacious Skinwillow. He shrugged. Neither of them liked to admit ignorance about anything at any time, but this was outside their experience. Both were lying in bed, looking out of the window at the seasonal and strange weather.

"Could it be a mirage?" she asked

"I think those only happen in deserts."

"Oh."

"Perhaps," Audacious Skinwillow said, "we all ate too many of those delicious and interesting mushrooms over the autumn."

"I ate none," she told him, "and yet I still see the black snowfall as clearly as I see you."

"Perhaps we are dreaming?" said Audacious Skinwillow.

Mrs Mallowfudge reached over and pinched his left testicle rather sharply.

"Aaah! Very well then, we are awake."

"We are certainly awake. And if we are neither dreaming nor hallucinating, there can only be one possibility left."

"And that would be?" he said.

"It is a sign."

"A sign?" he repeated, nursing his bruised appendage.

"A sign, and perhaps even a curse. This is a warning to us."

"What should we do?"

"Wait," said Mrs Mallowfudge, darkly. "And see."

Over the next two weeks, the black snow continued to fall, and the village became darker and darker until you could barely see it once night had come. There were a number of accidents: barked shins, heads knocked against walls, and several sprained ankles. The villagers began to stay in at night. When they did venture out, they went to the village pub, the Muddlenose Arms, where they reported all the odd and curious incidents they had experienced. Mr Barleygrow had lost his walking stick and found it several hours later, upside down in his garden. Louise Wandlesticks had seen a robin in the woods that refused to sing for her. Old Mrs Pettigram had suddenly taken an implacable dislike to bacon, formerly her favourite of all foods. The villagers muttered, and drank, and then muttered louder.

After some more drinking, the muttering became open discussion, and the theme of the discussion was: "What has changed since last year?" For, as Audacious Skinwillow pointed out, and all agreed, the snow had been the right and proper colour of White last winter, and nothing untoward had occurred at all. Indeed, as Mrs Mallowfudge asserted, and all further agreed, nothing strange had happened in Muddlenose for the whole time she had lived there, and that was a good fifty years. Old Mrs Pettigram was enlisted to confirm that the thirty years before that had also been entirely uneventful.

In short, the village was in an uproar, and the question asked over and over again with increasing force and meaning, was "What is different?" Finally, somebody - and they could never remember which of them it was but it could have been any one of the assembled throng - somebody said, "We have a stranger here now."

"Yes."

"Mr Glittergrime."

"A new arrival."

"Never speaks."

"Goes for long walks."

"Never smiles."

"And when he does it seems somehow menacing."

"I never hear any sound from his room," offered Miss Chasepaper. "Quiet as a mouse. Or as the grave."

"Or as the grave," someone repeated.

There was a moment of silence.

And then out of the blue and with a note of alarm that at once infected the rest of the pub, Old Mrs Pettigram said: "What if Christmas doesn't come this year?"

Suddenly everyone knew, knew for certain, that she was right. If snow could be black, then it was possible that Christmas would not come.

Muddlenose loved Christmas. Everyone gave everyone else a present, the old oak tree was hung with candles, and every house was decorated with red berries and green ivy. The preparations for Christmas were due to start tomorrow. But what would be the point if Christmas was not going to come?

A chill fell upon the villagers. "What if Christmas doesn't come?" they repeated softly.

Mrs Mallowfudge stood up with the light of prophecy in her eyes.

"Christmas will *not* come," she pronounced, as if she had heard it from the lips of Santa himself. "Christmas will not come this year, unless we find a cure for our curse." She paused, taking in the sight of the villagers with their eyes open as wide as mince pies. "We must heal ourselves, somehow."

Mr Barleygrow looked thoughtful. "I have some ointment at home," he offered. "It is supposed to be for rheumatism, but-"

"What we need is a priest," Miss Chasepaper said, more firmly. "We'll get the vicar to do an exorcism. Like in the Bible. Drive out the demon."

There was a pause while the villagers contemplated the idea of the elderly and vague Reverend Finkbottle conducting an exorcism to drive out a demon. There was a communal twitch at the corner of their mouths.

"Perhaps," said Mrs Pettigram timidly, "we could dye the snow white again? I have some bleach and a mop..."

Mrs Mallowfudge sighed and climbed on to a chair. "Listen," she called. They did. "I know what we have to do, to be safe. Trust me." She paused. "We have to offer a sacrifice."

There was silence, and a certain amount of shuffling. The villager's faces were blank. But Audacious stood up next to Mrs Mallowfudge, and he nodded vehemently. "We have an intruder," he said. "We have an interloper."

The villagers' faces were still blank, but beginning to be tinged with acceptance. Mr Glittergrime had done wrong to none of them, but he was undoubtedly a stranger, and if something had gone wrong with winter, it was perfectly logical to assume that he was, in some way, to blame.

One of the more enquiring Muddlenosians, ventured to ask the awkward but perhaps necessary question: "How did he do it?"

And that crystallised something in the people's minds, because they had not been sure till then whether he was a passive agent, unknowing, or an active agent, evil. Except for Mrs Mallowfudge and Audacious Skinwillow, who had known at once, or even before, that Mr Glittergrime was, in essence, and ultimately, bad. This knowledge was not based on events but on instinct: the unerring recognition of dark and light, which was conveniently typified by the black snow falling instead of white, and which could only be interpreted as a direct and unsubtle symbol whose meaning was of course Corruption.

"He cursed us," said the two village leaders together, both knowing it was true.

"He may be a demon," Audacious said, "or a servant of demons. Note how he cannot speak human language, and that he cringes when we approach. He walks in the woods at midnight."

"To *commune*," said Mrs Mallowfudge.

"And his diabolical conjurings have borne terrible fruit, as you can see all around you in the form of this black, black snow."

The villagers nodded, although they could not in fact actually see the snow because it was night-time. Yet they accepted it as a rhetorical device, and dutifully pictured their dark village, and shuddered. Muddlenose suddenly had the very whiff of demon.

With sudden fervour, Mr Barleygrow said, "I found his familiar! Last night, walking in the woods, I saw a figure built of snow, black snow, looming out of the darkness. It had the stench of evil about it."

There was a collective gasp.

"We face a crisis," said Mrs Mallowfudge, with all the authority at her command - and after thirty or so years as the unofficial but universally accepted village leader, that was a lot of authority. "We must deal with it swiftly, and strongly."

"So we must make a sacrifice to the spirit of Christmas?" said Miss Chasepaper, trying the idea out for size.

"And then Christmas will come, and the black snow will melt," said Mr Barleygrow hopefully.

"And then all will be back to normal."

"And we will be freed from this horrible weather."

"Yes," said Mrs Mallowfudge. "We will sacrifice the demon."

Everyone cheered.

Mr Glittergrime, needless to say, had not been in the pub. He was in his room, reading. He had been confused by the black snowfall, but this was his first winter in England, so he presumed that black snow was peculiar to the country, like smog. Nevertheless, he had come to enjoy the sensation of striding through crisp, dark snowdrifts and feeling black snowflakes falling on his head. He had even built a black snowman in the woods. He was contented.

He was therefore extremely confused to find an angry mob standing outside his window, throwing black snowballs against the glass and shouting. When he went downstairs and opened the front door, raising an enquiring eyebrow, he became further confused to find himself being dragged from the warm hallway out to the freezing road and from thence to the big oak tree by the church. The tree was a stark and cheerless object now, flinging its empty branches to the sky, almost crushed with the weight of the jet snow that covered it.

The villagers tied Mr Glittergrime to the tree. Then some of them went to their homes and fetched great bundles of ivy and candles to put in the branches, brightly coloured cloths to decorate the trunk, and they poured mead around the base of the tree so that it sank into the roots. They tore branches from the tree so that they would have light to see by, and flames lit up the churchyard. They adorned the Winter Tree for Christmas with Mr Glittergrime as the centrepiece, wrapped in red and green fabrics and bound with ivy. He did not resist. He asked, once, "What on earth is going on?" But he asked it in his own language, and since the villagers did not understand him, they pretended not to hear him.

Finally, the tree was ready, and they stood around it in solemn admiration for a few moments, ignoring the cold that crept into their arms and legs and noses.

"Christmas," said Audacious, flinging up his arms, "do not desert us!"

"Accept our tribute!" Mrs Mallowfudge said to the sky. "Not just the demon who would take you from us, but our Tree, which has stood here for as many years as any of us can remember, and will stand no longer. Take it! Accept it!"

And she took a flaming branch and set fire to the Winter Tree.

The oak was too green to burn well, but the smoky unsatisfying fire burned Mr. Glittergrime nonetheless. All of the adults of Muddlenose stood and watched in the dark. The passion they had worked up earlier in the warm, lit pub slowly melted away until all that was left was the darkness and the flames and the choking smoke. Still, they stood there till the end, as if warming their hands at a bonfire. But nobody's hands were warm.

When the fire finally burned out, Mr. Glittergrime was dead – most likely from the smoke, although no one could stand to look at his blackened body for long enough to tell.

And then morning came.

Mrs Mallowfudge and Audacious Skinwillow tried to whip Muddlenose into a sensation of triumph and accomplishment, but they met with little success. When Reverend Finkbottle emerged from the vicarage, Mrs Pettigram quickly engaged him in conversation and led him away so that he would not see their shame: for the villagers knew now that it was shame they felt.

The children came out of their houses and started to run around, but their parents shushed them and sent them back inside. The villagers grimly cut down their victim and laid him in the snow, where his naked body was so charred that it became camouflaged by the snow. The villagers shut his eyes and crossed his hands.

And then they dispersed to their homes, or to the woods, and were quiet. The pub was deserted. Nobody went near the remains of the Winter Tree, and nobody put up any decorations. Except for Mrs Mallowfudge, who defiantly strung a row of brightly coloured paper lanterns across her front garden, and found them trampled only an hour later.

Two mornings after the Winter Tree Sacrifice, Mrs Mallowfudge and Audacious Skinwillow left the village. They did it silently, without goodbyes. They packed suitcases, stole a horse and cart, and disappeared. In fact, they only went as far as the next village, Hayfeather, which was slightly larger, but the effect was to remove them as thoroughly as if they had died. Occasional rumours floated back – that one of them had murdered the other, that both had suffocated themselves in the snow, that they had opened a hat shop together – but even though Muddlenose liked its gossip, they did not pursue the rumours. The couple had gone, and no one mourned them.

But the villagers mourned Mr Glittergrime, whose real name they never knew. On the day that Mrs Mallowfudge and Audacious Skinwillow left, Muddlenose held a funeral for him under the name they had given him, and his gravestone said the same.

The day after that was Christmas Eve, and then, finally, they put up Christmas decorations and roasted their turkeys and mulled their wine, and Christmas came as usual. (For, as Mrs Pettigram remarked to Mr Barleygrow in a shamefaced whisper, how could it not come, when they created it themselves? A fact that had not previously occurred to them.)

The next year, the snow was white, and Muddlenose never did find out why they had had the year of black snow. But in the years that followed, on every Christmas Eve, the entire village would gather by the churchyard, by the stump of the Winter Tree, and they would bring a feast: plum puddings, apple tarts, roast chickens, mince pies, jugs of cider and mead. They would decorate one of the trees in the churchyard with ivy and berries, and they would eat and drink in the cold, with a fire to keep themselves warm. When they had finished eating, they would scrape some of the ashes from the fire and sprinkle them over one of the graves in the churchyard so that it looked as if the snow had turned black.

Then at midnight, someone would take the last jug of mead, which was always kept back for this purpose, and they would pour it, slowly and silently, on to the black grave. They would contemplate for a few moments the wet and snowy gravestone and the Winter Tree Sacrifice. They would remember Mr Glittergrime, whose name they never knew, and would never forget.

~~~~~

The Wood

I have a confession to make, Grandfather. I walked through the woods today. I was on my way to see you, and it was getting dark, and I took the shortcut through the woods, just as you always warned me not to do.

I turned off the path and went among the dark trees, trusting that I could find my way to you. I sang to avert danger and I walked quickly, not looking too closely to left or to right, because you have told me stories of what lives in the woods and I did not want to find out that you were right.

But you were right, Grandfather. And now I have met the things who live in your woods.

At first there was nothing, no sound at all. The wood was thick and enclosing, but it was still light, and I walked briskly. The silence was first reassuring, and then oppressive. I sang more loudly to overcome it.

After a few minutes, I heard a noise I had not expected. Something was purring. When I turned, there was an animal peering from behind a large oak tree. Not a cat, but like a cat. It had no tail and stood on its hind legs, and its whiskers and fur were russet-red.

"Child," it said to me, still purring while it spoke, "come into the heart of the wood with me."

"I will not," I said, "because my Grandfather who tends these woods has warned me against you."

"Has he indeed? That weak old man who lives in the broken-down cottage? And what did he say?"

"He said that your bite is poison, and you would try to trap me among the trees and strip off my skin to keep you warm."

"But he is wrong," purred the cat-thing, "because I have fur already and I would not need your skin for warmth."

"Perhaps you are right," I said, "but still I will not go with you into the heart of the wood."

The cat bowed to me, and vanished among the trees.

I walked on and the trees sighed around me, and the wood became darker and colder. After a while I stopped to sit down by a tree for a rest, and as I sat a creature appeared in front of me. It was like a large sheep, but shorn, and its eyes were amber.

"Come with me into the heart of the wood," it said in a high voice.

"I will not," I said, "because my grandfather has told me about you."

"That lonely old man in the tumble-down cottage who believes he has charge of the wood? And what did he say?"

"He said you would take me into the heart of the wood and suck my blood away, and leave me dry under the trees."

The sheep-thing bared its teeth at me and I saw they were blunt. "He lied to you," it said, "because you can see I could not drink your blood with these small teeth."

"Perhaps you are right, but I still will not go with you to the heart of the wood."

The creature bowed politely to me, and disappeared among the trees.

After a few minutes I walked on, deeper and deeper into the wood, and I began to worry that I would never reach your cottage, Grandfather, because I seemed to have been walking for hours. I stopped, trying to decide if I should turn back. At that moment there was a noise somewhere away from the path, and then a noise behind me, and when I turned round there was a fox-creature looking at me. It was much bigger than ordinary foxes, and midnight black all over so that I could only just see it against the wood's blackness, but its eyes were bright green. My knees shook under me, but I looked back at it steadily.

"Come with me into the heart of the wood, human child," said the black fox, in a low and gentle voice.

"My grandfather did not tell me about you," I said, uncertainly.

"That wise old man who looks after the forest?" said the fox sweetly. "Perhaps he did not think you would ever meet me. For I live at the heart of the wood and I never stray far from it."

I thought back to your many tales and warnings, Grandfather, and I remembered something you had told me, once, late at night by the dim glow of your fading fire. "Grandfather told me," I said quietly, "that there was something at the wood's heart that wanted to take me and dig out my brain and my heart and replace them with its own, and then I would become like a wild animal. But I did not believe him."

"You are a wise child, for I have never seen anything like that in my wood," said the fox. "Come with me, my dear child, for you are cold and tired and without me you will never find your way to your grandfather's cottage." His fur looked warm and soft and his green eyes kind.

Grandfather, you are shivering. Let me put another blanket on your lap. Is my story entertaining you? Come, smile at me, smile for your granddaughter.

You want to know if I went with the black fox? No, no, of course not. I bade him goodbye and continued on my way, and eventually I found my way here, and here I am. If I had gone with him, he would have taken my brain and my heart and devoured them and replaced them with his own, and then I would be nothing but a wild animal covered in human flesh, and I would leap on you and eat you, and leave nobody to look after the wood. And that would be terrible.

But that did not happen. Why would you not believe me? I am your own loving granddaughter.

Yes, Grandfather, of course my eyes were always this colour.

No, Grandfather, you cannot examine my hands.

Oh, my dear Grandfather, do please stop screaming.

~~~~~

Squirrel Killing

I sat in my room and thought about blood.

It had been, frankly, a boring day. Long and boring. The only thing to eat in the flat was chicken, my wound was hurting, and I'd slept from midday to four o'clock just because I couldn't think of anything else to do. My wound is in my leg and it hurts when the sun is shining, like today. I had a car accident four years ago when I was young; I recovered. It was my fault, I ran in front of the car. David nursed me back to health, stayed off work to do so.

I don't like chicken.

But the chicken came in one of those foam trays, the ones you have to tear apart when you've eaten, because that's the most interesting part of the whole process. And the tray had what David calls "chicken juice" in it. Blood, in other words: David's a little squeamish, unlike me. So I sat on the floor and looked at the blood and thought about killing something.

Not a person, I don't have the strength for that. I know my own weaknesses. A thing. A rodent, probably. I know: you're thinking I don't have much ambition, why not a dog or a fox? But I don't want to overreach myself, think how David would feel if I came home bleeding, with an eye ripped out or something. He'd feel terrible. I'd feel terrible. Best to stick to what I know.

I went out, thinking that I needed at least a walk, even if no blood came of it. I prowled down the street, making sure to avoid the cars: it's one of those back roads that cars come down very fast, because the alternative, main route is always busy and has sleeping policemen all over it. Someone's going to get killed on this road. One of the children who go to the school that's on the corner. One of the adults who pick them up after school's finished. One of the pets who roam the streets at night. Me.

The driver will be distraught, I suppose. I don't know much about how drivers think. I'm essentially a pedestrian.

There was a squirrel on the corner, in the big tree: I don't know what type of tree it is, not my area of expertise. It was a grey squirrel. David says they're pests, but he likes to watch them. If one runs across the road in front of him, he'll stay very still and try to coax it over. God knows why. People always want these furry scampering things to *like* them, don't they? As if there was any reason why an animal should look at a human with anything other than terror. The squirrel always runs away, because David's quite intimidating, tall and broad and with a thick beard. And a Yorkshire accent, not that I would expect the squirrel to notice or care about that. I rather like it myself.

I stayed very still, crouched on the pavement. I checked that nobody was watching. The squirrel ran down the tree.

I'm not intimidating. The squirrel gradually came nearer to me, scurrying backwards and forwards in that cute way they have. Furry, and swishing its thick tail in what seemed to be an overture of friendship – rodents actually do seem to take to me. (Is a squirrel a rodent? I've always assumed so.) I killed it easily, and ate a little bit of it. I'd like to kill more slowly, but I just can't help myself. They always die the moment I grab them by the throat. David says I don't know my own strength.

I won't tell him about the squirrel of course: he's be horrified. He doesn't mind the occasional mouse, as long as I wash myself carefully afterwards, but no more than that.
Squeamish, as I said. Not like me. I don't call it squirrel juice:

I know it's blood, it's all blood. The most important substance in the world.

I washed very carefully this time, licking myself all over. No traces of squirrel blood were left. I loved the taste of squirrel blood, by the way. It was my first experience of it, and I found it to be definitely different from, say, vole blood – "vole juice" as David might say. It was almost magical: I thought pixie blood might taste that way, an unusually fey thought for me. I must have been accidentally reading some of those New Age magazines David leaves on the floor. Normally I just sit on them, the parts he wants to read. I want all of his attention all the time, you see. Like a baby, he says sometimes. I cuddle up against him when he's on the phone and make him stroke me, and I lick his face, and both of us are happy. And why not?

I left the remains of the squirrel in the back garden. I'm sure David won't associate it with me. Then I curled up and slept again.

He came home at six, as usual.

"How was your day, dear?" he said, as usual.

"Fine, dear," I said, taking his coat. "I cleaned the bathroom, and I've made you dinner."

"Thanks, darling. Anything interesting happen? I worry about you, here all day, just doing housework. I want you to enjoy yourself."

"Oh," I said, "don't worry, darling. I do."

Kate Harrad is a London-based writer whose first novel, *All Lies and Jest*, is being published by Ghostwoods Books. She likes kittens and rainbows, but for some reason prefers to write about misguided ritual sacrifices and mutated roadkill.

Kate's website is at loveandzombies.co.uk.